First French

AT SCHOOL

Kathy Gemmell and Jenny Tyler
Illustrated by Sue Stitt
Designed by Diane Thistlethwaite

Consultants: Sarah-Lou Reekie and Kate Griffin

CONTENTS

First published in 1993 by Usborne Publishing Ltd.
Usborne House, 83-85 Saffron Hill
London EC1N 8RT, England.
Copyright © 1993 Usborne Publishing Ltd.

Printed in Portugal. UE

First published in America March 1994

Speaking French

This book is about the Noisette [nwa zet] family. They are going to help you learn to speak French.

Word lists

You will find a word list on each double page to tell you what the French words mean.

Bonjour
bonjoor

Word list

bonjour bonjoor	hello
salut salew	hi
je m'appelle je mapell	I am called
l'oncle lonkl	uncle
pardon pardaw	sorry
à toi ah twa	your turn
où est le chat? oo ai le sha	where is the cat?

Salut
salew

The little letters are to help you say the French words. Read them as if they were English words.

Je m'appelle Henri.
je mapell onree

Je m'appelle Oncle Paul.
je mapell onkl pol

Où est le chat?
oo ai le sha

Pardon
pardaw

The best way to find out how to say French words is to listen to a French person speaking. Some sounds are different from English. Here are some clues to help you.

When you see a "j" in French, say it like the middle sound in "treasure". Try saying *je*, which means "I".

When you see an "n" in French, be careful. Single "n"s are hardly pronounced. Only double "n"s or "n"s which come before a,e,i,o or u are pronounced.

To say the "u" in *salut*, round your lips to say "oo" then say "ee" instead.

Say the French "r" by making a rolling sound in the back of your mouth, a bit like gargling.

Try saying out loud what each person on this page is saying.

See if you can find Delphine the mouse on each double page.

Games with word lists

You can play games with the word lists if you like. Here are some ideas.

1. Cover all the English words and see if you can say the English for each French word. Score a point for each one you can remember.

2. Time yourself and see if you can say the whole list more quickly next time.

3. Race a friend. The first one to say the English for each word scores a point. The winner is the one to score the most points.

4. Play all these games the other way around, saying the French for each English word.

À toi
Look for the *à toi* [ah twa] boxes in this book. There is something for you to do in each of them. À toi means "your turn".

Look out for the joke bubbles on some of the pages.

3

In the classroom

Sophie and Henri Noisette are back at school today. There is a new boy in their class. He introduces himself by saying *Je m'appelle Marc* [je mapell mark]. *Je m'appelle* is how you say "I am called" or "my name is" in French.

Can you help the children introduce themselves to Marc, by saying what's in each speech bubble? Use the word list to help you.

Can you work out which way Marc should go so that he only passes each of them once and ends up at the teacher's desk?

Names

Noisette nwa zet	**Jean** jon
Chiffre sheefr	**Marc** mark
Roger ro jay	**Florence** flor onss
Sophie sofee	**Marie** maree
Henri onree	**Philippe** fee leep
Francine fronseen	**Pierre** pe air

Word list

comment tu t'appelles? kommaw tew tapell	what's your name?
je m'appelle je mapell	I am called/my name is
il s'appelle eel sapell	he is called
elle s'appelle el sapell	she is called
ma mère ma mair	my mother
mon père maw pair	my father
mon frère maw frair	my brother
ma sœur ma ser	my sister
Monsieur miss yer	Mr.
Madame ma dam	Mrs.
la grand-mère la gronmair	grandma

Happy families

Can you match up the people in the column on the right with the person who is talking about them? Use the word list to see what all the words mean.

What is Henri's sister called?
What is Sophie's father called?
Can you answer in French? *Il s'appelle* [eel sapell] means "he is called" and *elle s'appelle* [el sapell] means "she is called".

À toi

Comment tu t'appelles? [kommaw tew tapell]. What's your name? Try and introduce yourself and your family in French, using the words on this page to help you.

How are you?

Look at the picture to see how everyone is this morning.

To ask how someone is in French you say *Comment ça va?* [kommaw sa va] or sometimes just *Ça va?* [sa va] which means, "How are you?"

Madame Chiffre is talking to someone who is saying, "I'm very well, thank you," in French. Use the word list to see how to say this out loud.

Where are they?

Can you spot the following people in the picture?

Someone who has toothache?

Someone with a headache?

Someone who is saying, "My leg hurts"?

Someone with a tummy-ache?

Someone who feels all right?

Use the word list to help you say out loud in French what each person is saying.

Can you spot the words for hand, foot and arm on this page?

le bras
le bra

le pied
le pee ay

At home

Here are some of the Noisette family at home. They should be saying how they feel but the speech bubbles have all been mixed up. Can you say what each person should be saying?

Madame Noisette

Grand-mère Noisette

Bonjour, ça va?

Ça va très bien, merci.

Ça va?

Ça va?

J'ai mal aux dents.

Ça va bien, merci.

la main
la ma

J'ai mal à la jambe.

Ça va très bien.

Monsieur Noisette

Roger

Word list

bonjour bonjoor	good morning, hello
merci mairsee	thank you
(comment) ça va? kommaw sa va	how are you?
ça va bien sa va bee ai	I'm fine, I'm all right
ça va très bien sa va trai bee ai	I'm very well
j'ai mal aux dents jay mal oh daw	I have toothache
j'ai mal à la tête jay mal ala tet	I have a headache
j'ai mal au ventre jay mal oh vontr	I have a tummy-ache
j'ai mal à la·jambe jay mal ala jomb	my leg hurts
la grand-mère la gronmair	grandma
Madame ma dam	Mrs.
Monsieur miss yer	Mr.

Le and *la*

Can you see the words *le* and *la* on this page? These both mean "the" in French.

In French, all naming words (nouns) are either masculine or feminine. You use *le* for masculine words and *la* for feminine words. You cannot guess which is which, so you have to learn words with their *le* or *la*.

Before a word starting with a,e,i,o or u, you only say the first *l* of *le* or *la*.

À toi
Comment ça va? [kommaw sa va].
How *do* you feel at the moment? Look at what everyone in the cloakroom is saying to help you say how you feel today. Ask your family and friends how they are in French. You could draw pictures of them and give them French speech bubbles.

Counting

Can you help Sophie with her counting? Look at the first picture to see her counting books. Count the things in the other pictures in the same way, starting with *un* [a], *deux* [deuh].

How many things are in each picture? Answer by saying *il y a* [eel ya] and then the number of things you have counted. Use the word list to see how to say all the words.

Un, deux, trois, quatre, cinq, six, sept, huit, neuf, dix.

Il y a dix livres.

les livres

les plantes

les parapluies

Number list

un	one	cinq	five	huit	eight
a		sank		weet	
deux	two	six	six	neuf	nine
deuh		seess		neuf	
trois	three	sept	seven	dix	ten
trwa		set		deess	
quatre	four				
katr					

Word list

il y a	there is, there are	les chapeaux	hats
eel ya		lay shapo	
les livres	books	les plantes	plants
lay leevr		lay plont	
les crayons	pencils	les cadeaux	presents
lay krayaw		lay kado	
les parapluies	umbrellas		
lay para plewee			

Les means "the" when you are talking about more than one object (plural). You don't say *les* after a number.

À toi

Look for things around your house to count. Count them in French. If you want to continue past ten, here are the numbers up to twenty:

onze	eleven	seize	sixteen
onz		sez	
douze	twelve	dix-sept	seventeen
dooz		deesset	
treize	thirteen	dix-huit	eighteen
trez		deezweet	
quatorze	fourteen	dix-neuf	nineteen
katorz		deezneuf	
quinze	fifteen	vingt	twenty
kanz		va	

les cadeaux

Song

Here are the first three verses of a French song. Can you sing it right up to *Dix chats veulent manger...* using all the numbers up to ten in French? Sing it to the tune of "One man went to mow". You can see the tune on page 32 if you don't know it.

Un chat veut manger, veut manger du gâteau,
a sha veuh mawjay veuh mawjay dew ga toe
Un chat et son maître veulent manger du gâteau.
a sha ay saw metr veul maw jay dew ga toe

Deux chats veulent manger, veulent manger
deuh sha veul mawjay veul mawjay
du gâteau,
dew ga toe
Deux chats, un chat et son maître veulent
deuh sha a sha ay saw metr veul
manger du gâteau.
mawjay dew ga toe

Trois chats veulent manger, veulent manger
trwa sha veul mawjay veul mawjay
du gâteau,
dew ga toe
Trois chats, deux chats, un chat et son maître
trwa sha deuh sha a sha ay saw metr
veulent manger du gâteau.
veul mawjay dew ga toe

Here is what it means in English:

One cat wants to eat, wants to eat some cake
One cat and his master want to eat some cake.
Two cats want to eat ...etc.

les crayons

les chapeaux

Qu'est-ce que tu as si
kess ke tew a see
tu croises un éléphant
tew krwaz an ay lay faw
avec un kangourou?
avek a kongaroo

Des
day
trous énormes
troo aynorm
en Australie.
on ostralee

Joke: What do you get if you cross an elephant with a kangaroo?
Big holes in Australia.

Days of the week

Sophie and Henri both have timetables to tell them which subject their group will be doing each day.

Using Sophie and Henri's timetables, can you see which day it is in each of the pictures? Say *c'est* [sai] which means "it is" and then the day of the week. Look at the word list to see how to say each of the days.

Sophie	
lundi	dessin
mardi	français
mercredi	sport
jeudi	anglais
vendredi	musique
samedi	le week-end
dimanche	

Henri	
lundi	sport
mardi	dessin
mercredi	anglais
jeudi	français
vendredi	musique
samedi	le week-end
dimanche	

Word list

c'est *sai*	it is
lundi *lundee*	Monday
mardi *mardee*	Tuesday
mercredi *mairkredee*	Wednesday
jeudi *jeuh dee*	Thursday
vendredi *vondredee*	Friday
samedi *samdee*	Saturday
dimanche *deemonsh*	Sunday
le week-end *le week end*	weekend
le français *le fronsai*	French
l'anglais *longlai*	English
le sport *le spor*	sport
le dessin *le dessa*	drawing, art
la musique *la mewzeek*	music

The days of the week do not have capital letters in French.

How many times can you spot the word *le* on these two pages? Remember, *le* is how you say "the" when you are talking about masculine words. For feminine words, "the" is *la*.

A

B

My name is Sophie.

A

B

Il y a deux chapeaux.

D

Il y a trois chapeaux.

C

D

Indoor hopscotch

Hopscotch in French is called *la marelle* [la marell]. Here is a type of hopscotch you can play indoors.

Using the word list to help you, write out the days of the week in French on seven squares of paper (each one large enough to put your foot on).

The aim of the game is to collect as many of the paper squares as possible.

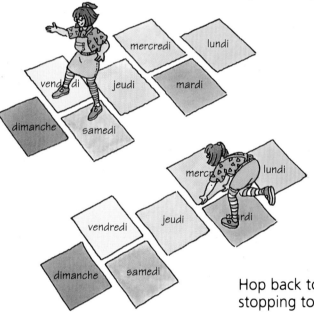

Arrange the seven squares on the floor like this with *lundi* (Monday) nearest you:

Stand about 1m (3ft) away from the first square. Throw a coin onto any one of the squares. Say that day out loud in French, using *c'est* and then the day. (If the stone lands between or outside the squares, throw again.)

Then hop up the squares, putting one foot on each of the squares that are side by side, without stepping on the square with the stone on it. You can only hop once on the top square (*dimanche*).

Hop back to the beginning, stopping to pick up the coin and its paper square on the way.

Continue until you have thrown the coin onto all the squares. Remember to say each of the days out loud in French. You will have to hop over wider and wider gaps as you pick up more and more squares.

You can play this game by yourself, or with a friend. If you are playing with a friend, take turns to throw. The winner is the one with the most paper squares at the end.

Joke: Waiter, there's a spider in my soup!
I'm sorry, sir, it's the fly's day off.

À toi
Can you say in French what day it is today? Remember, say *c'est* [sai] then the day.
Try saying what day it is in French every morning for a week.

11

Putting on a play

Everyone is getting ready for the school play. Most of the children seem to have lost something in the piles of clothes lying around the stage.

To say, "I have lost," in French, say *j'ai perdu* [jay pairdew] and then what you have lost.

Using the word list to help you, can you say in French what each child is saying? *Mon* [maw], *ma* [ma] and *mes* [may] all mean "my".

Can you find all the lost objects? Point to each one and say, "there it is" or "there they are". This is *le voilà* [le vwala] for *le* words (the ones with *mon* before them), *la voilà* [la vwala] for *la* words (the ones with *ma* before them) or *les voilà* [lay vwala] for the words with *mes* before them (plural).

12

Word list

j'ai perdu *jay pairdew*	I have lost	**mon crayon** *maw krayaw*	my pencil
mes gants *may gaw*	my gloves	**ma trousse** *ma trooss*	my pencil case
ma ceinture *ma santewr*	my belt	**mes feutres** *may feutr*	my felt tips
ma montre *ma montr*	my watch	**mon cahier** *maw kaeeay*	my exercise book
mon gilet *maw jeelay*	my cardigan	**et** *ay*	and
mes lunettes *may lewnet*	my glasses	**le/la voilà** *le/la vwala*	there it is
mon chapeau *maw shapo*	my hat	**les voilà** *lay vwala*	there they are

À toi

Here is a French memory game that you can play with two or more players. One person starts by saying *j'ai perdu* [jay pairdew] and then the name of an object in French. You can use any of the objects on this page.

Take turns repeating what the person before has said and then adding another object to the list. To say "and " in French, you say *et* [ay]. You are out if you can't remember everything in the right order or can't think of an object to add. The winner is the last one to be out.

Art class

Francine has painted a picture of an animal she particularly likes, using her favourite colour.

Look how she says which colour and animal she likes best.

Can you see which is Francine's painting?

Use the word list to help you match each of Francine's friends with their pictures.

Word list

mon animal préféré est.. mon anee mal prai fai rai ai	my favourite animal is..
ma couleur préférée est le/l'.. ma kooler prai fai rai ai le	my favourite colour is..
le chat le sha	the cat
le chien le sheea	the dog
le lapin le lapa	the rabbit
la souris la sooree	the mouse
le cheval le shval	the horse
l'éléphant laylayfaw	the elephant
le cochon le ko shaw	the pig

One animal on the word list isn't anyone's favourite. Can you spot which one it is?

Ma couleur préférée est l'orange. Mon animal préféré est le cheval.

Ma couleur préférée est le jaune. Mon animal préféré est le lapin.

Ma couleur préférée est le marron. Mon anima préféré est la souris.

À toi

Tell someone in French what colour you like best. Try saying what your favourite animal is. You can use what Francine's friends are saying to help you.

Pourquoi les
poorkwa laze
éléphants sont-ils
aylayfaw sonteel
grands et gris?
graw ay gree

Parce que s'ils
parss ke seelz
étaient petits et blancs,
aitai ptee ay blaw
ils seraient des flocons
eel serai day flokaw
de neige.
de nej

Ma couleur
préférée est le vert.
Mon animal préféré
est le chat.

Ma couleur
préférée est le rouge.
Mon animal préféré
est le chien.

Ma couleur
préférée est le bleu.
Mon animal préféré
est le cochon.

Colour guide

bleu (bleue)
bleuh
rouge
rooj
vert (verte)
vair, vairt
orange
oronj
jaune
jone
violet (violette)
vee o lay, vee o let
blanc (blanche)
blaw, blonsh
noir (noire)
nwar
marron
marraw

French colour words often
change slightly when they
are used to describe particular
objects. You use the first word
above to describe masculine *le*
things. The words in brackets
describe feminine *la* things.
On this page, you use the first
word on the guide.

15

Joke: Why are elephants big and grey?
Because if they were small and white they'd be snowflakes.

French calendar

Sophie and her friends are making French calendars which last for twelve years. You can make one too by following the instructions below.

Use the word list to find out the names of the months in French. Look back at page 10 if you can't remember which day of the week is which.

1. Use the ruler to draw 3cm (1in) squares over one of the sheets of cardboard, then cut the sheet into strips lengthwise (each strip 3cm (1in) wide).

2. Each strip will have just over nine squares on it. On the first strip, leave one full blank square at either end, then write in the days of the week in French, one on each square, like this:

You will need:
2 sheets of cardboard about 29cm by 21cm (11in by 8in), scissors, pencils and felt tip pens, a ruler and some glue.

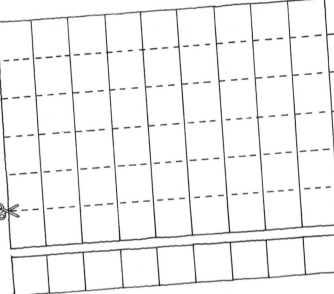

| lundi | mardi | mercredi | jeudi | vendredi | samedi | dimanche |

3. Stick the next two strips together to make one very long strip and mark numbers 1-16 on one side, again leaving a blank square at either end. Don't cut these off. Draw 3cm (1in) squares on the other side and write in numbers 17-31.

| 1 | 2 | 3 | 4 | 5 | 6 | 7 | 8 | 9 | 10 | 11 | 12 | 13 | 14 | 15 | 16 |

| 17 | 18 | 19 | 20 | 21 | 22 | 23 | 24 | 25 | 26 | 27 | 28 | 29 | 30 | 31 | |

Word list

janvier *jonveeay*	January	juillet *jooeeay*	July	l'hiver *leevair*	winter
février *fave reeay*	February	août *oot*	August	le printemps *le prantaw*	spring
mars *marss*	March	septembre *septombr*	September	l'été *laitai*	summer
avril *avreel*	April	octobre *octobr*	October	l'automne *lo tonn*	autumm
mai *may*	May	novembre *novombr*	November		
juin *jwah*	June	décembre *daysombr*	December	French people don't spell months, seasons, nor days of the week with capital letters.	

4. On the next strip write the months in French: *janvier* to *juin* on one side and *juillet* to *décembre* on the other. This time you will have more than one square left over. Don't cut them off as you will need them to pull the strips through the calendar.

5. The last strip is for the years. Write 1993 to 1998 on one side and 1999 to 2004 on the other.

6. Mark off the second sheet as shown below:

Cut slots along the lines. Thread your strips through to show the right day, date, month and year.

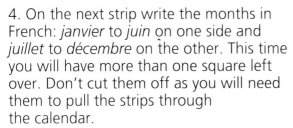

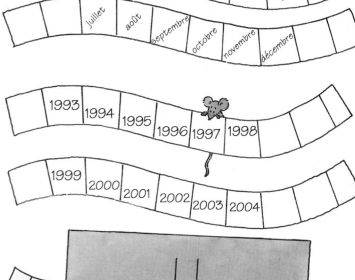

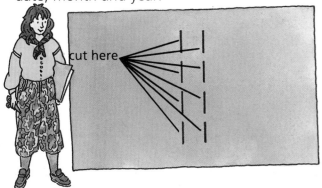

Sophie and the others are decorating an enormous calendar they have made for the classroom. You could decorate the front of your calendar too, using the different seasons.

Comment
kommaw
s'appelle un bébé qui
sappela baibai kee
est né en mars?
ai nayaw marss

Un martien
a marsseea

Joke: What do you call a baby born in March? A martian.

What is it?

Madame Chiffre has divided the class into teams to play a guessing game. The teams wear blindfolds and take turns to pick objects out of a large box. They must guess what they have picked out.

To ask what something is in French, you say *est-ce que c'est...?* [ess ke sai], which means "is it...?" and then the name of the object.

To answer, you say *oui, c'est...* [wee sai], which means "yes, it's...", or *non, ce n'est pas...* [naw, se nai pa], which means "no, it's not...".

Using the word list to help you, can you answer everyone's questions?

Can you now tell the people who have guessed wrongly what their objects are, using *c'est* [sai] and then the name of the object? So you would say to Sophie, *C'est un coquillage* [sait a kokeeaj].

Word list

est-ce que c'est...? *ess ke sai*	is it...?	une sucette *ewn sewset*	a lollipop
oui *wee*	yes	un cerf-volant *a sair volaw*	a kite
non *naw*	no	un coquillage *a kokeeaj*	a shell
c'est *sai*	it is	un livre *a leevr*	a book
ce n'est pas *se nai pa*	it is not	une montre *ewn montr*	a watch
un pipeau *a peepo*	a recorder	un porte-monnaie *a port monay*	a purse
un sifflet *a seeflay*	a whistle	un crayon *a krayaw*	a pencil
une raquette *ewn rackett*	a racket		

Est-ce que c'est une sucette?

Oui, c'est une sucette.

Est-ce que c'est un porte-monnaie?

Est-ce que c'est un livre?

Est-ce que c'est un pipeau?

Est-ce que c'est un pipeau?

Non, ce n'est pas un pipeau.

Song

Here is a song to sing in French. Can you guess what any of the words mean? You can check what they all mean on page 32.

Qu'est-ce que c'est que je vois là? Est-ce que c'est un gros vieux rat?
kess ke sai ke je vwa la ess ke sait a grow veeyeuh ra

Ce n'est pas un poiss - on rouge, ni un é - lé - phant qui bouge,
Se nai paz a pwass aw rooj nee an ay lay faw kee booj

Qu'est-ce que c'est que je vois là? Ça va, c'est mon pe - tit chat.
kess ke sai ke je vwa la sa va sai maw peuh tee sha

Joke: What has eight legs, two wheels and goes very fast?
A spider on a motorbike.

Hide and seek

During break, Francine and Henri are playing hide and seek. It's Henri's turn to hide. Can you spot him? (If you can't remember who Henri is, look back to page 5.)

To say, "There he is," in French, you say *Le voilà* [le vwala].

Où est Francine? [oo ai fronseen]. Where is Francine? To say, "There she is", you say *La voilà* [la vwala].

Can you find which paths Francine must take to reach Henri by the shortest route? She cannot use any of the paths which are blocked by children or objects.

Word list

où est oo ai	where is
le voilà le vwala	there he, it is
la voilà la vwaia	there she, it is
le drapeau le dra po	flag
le chat le sha	cat
la souris la sooree	mouse
le vélo le vaylo	bicycle
le cerf-volant le sair volaw	kite
le jardinier le jardeeneeay	gardener

Can you spot some other things in the picture? Say *Le voilà* [le vwala] when you spot a *le* object and *La voilà* when you find a *la* object.

Où est le cerf-volant?

Où est le chat?

Où est le vélo?

Où est le drapeau?

Où est la souris?

Joke: What goes thththth?
A snake with a lisp.

Tongue twister

How fast can you say this tongue twister without making any mistakes?

Un chasseur sachant
a shasser sashaw
chasser doit savoir chasser
shassay dwah savvar shassay
sans son chien.
saw saw sheea

Here is what it means in English: *A hunter who knows how to hunt should know how to hunt without his dog.*

21

Sports day

Today is sports day. Madame Chiffre is asking who knows how to climb, *Qui sait grimper?* [kee sai grampay]. Sophie answers, *Je sais grimper* [je sais grampay] which means, "I know how to climb".

Use the word list opposite to help you answer these questions for the people in the picture. Point to someone who is doing each activity and say *je sais* [je sai] for them and then what he or she is doing.

Qui sait faire le poirier?
Qui sait courir?
Qui sait ramper?
Qui sait faire des cabrioles?
Qui sait faire la roue?
Qui sait marcher à cloche-pied?
Qui sait sauter?

Qui sait grimper?

Je sais grimper.

Monsieur le docteur,
missyer le doctur
l'homme invisible
lom anvee zeebl
vous attend.
vooz attaw

Dites-lui que je
deet lwee ke je
ne peux pas le voir.
ne peuh pa le vwar

À toi
Do you know how to do any of the things in the picture? Look at the word list to see how to say what you can do in French. Remember, say *je sais* [je sai] and then what you can do.

22

Joke: Doctor, the invisible man's waiting for you. Tell him that I can't see him.

Word list

qui sait...? *kee sai*	who can/knows how...?	faire des cabrioles *fair day kabreeole*	to do somersaults
je sais *je sai*	I can/know how	marcher à cloche-pied *marshay a klosh pee ay*	to hop
sais-tu...? *sai tew*	can you...?	ramper *rompay*	to crawl
courir *kooreer*	to run	grimper *grampay*	to climb
faire le poirier *fair le pwareeay*	to do a handstand	sauter *so tay*	to jump
faire la roue *fair la roo*	to do a cartwheel		

French flip-flaps

Here is how to make and use a French flip-flap.

You will need:

a large square of paper and some felt tips.

Fold each corner of your paper square into the middle. Turn the paper over and do the same on the other side.

Write numbers 2 to 9, one on each of the small triangles you can now see.

Lift up the four flaps in turn. Under each number, write down *sais-tu* [sai tew], which means "can you" followed by one of the activites from the word list. You will have to write in little writing to fit in all the words.

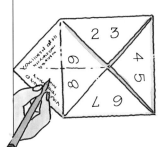

Fold the flaps in again and turn the square back over.

Write *bleu, rouge, jaune* and *vert* on the four small squares. Fill them in with your felt tips. (Look back at page 14 if you can't remember which ones to use).

Slide both your index fingers and thumbs under the squares and push them together like this:

Ask a friend to choose a square. Say the word on it, then do this as you spell it out:

Now ask your friend to choose a number. Count it out in French, opening your flip-flap to the top and side as before. (If you can't remember all the numbers in French, look back at page 8.)

When you finish counting, ask your friend to choose another number. This time, open up that flap and read out loud in French what it says under the number your friend has chosen. Your friend must do the activity you read, or start again.

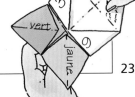

Lunchtime

Today, lunch is outside. Unfortunately, not everyone seems to be having a good time.

Cathy [katee] is in a bad mood because she has ripped her skirt. *Je suis de mauvaise humeur* [je swee de mo vaze ewmur] means, "I am in a bad mood," in French.

How do you think the other children are feeling? Use the word list to help you match each speech bubble below with a child in the picture. Can you say each one out loud in French?

> J'ai soif.

> J'ai faim.

> J'ai chaud.

> J'ai froid.

> J'ai soif.

> J'ai faim.

> Je suis content.

> Je suis fatigué.

> J'ai faim.

> Je suis triste.

À toi

How do you feel at the moment?

Use the word list to describe how you feel in French. Remember to use the extra "e" on the end of the words for happy and tired if you are a girl.

24

Joke: Give me the names of 30 animals which come from Africa.
29 elephants and a giraffe.

Word list

In French, some describing words (adjectives) are slightly different for boys and girls. Where there are two words together on this list, use the first to describe a boy and the second to describe a girl.

French	Pronunciation	English
j'ai faim	jay fa	I'm hungry
j'ai soif	jay swaf	I'm thirsty
j'ai chaud	jay show	I'm hot
j'ai froid	jay frwa	I'm cold
je suis	je swee	I am

French	Pronunciation	English
content, contente	kontaw, kontont	happy
triste	treest	sad
fatigué, fatiguée	fateegay, fateegay	tired
de mauvaise humeur	de mo vaze ewmur	in a bad mood

Telling the time

Suzanne must meet Sophie and Francine from school today but her watch is broken so she has to keep asking the time.

To ask the time in French, you say *Quelle heure est-il?* [keller aiteel]. To answer, you say *il est* [eel ai] which means "it is" and then the time.

Heures [ur] after a number on the clock means "o'clock".

So to say, "It's 10 o'clock," in French, you say *Il est dix heures* [eel ai deezer]. How do you say, "It's six o'clock"?

Can you say *Il est ... heures* for each of the hours on Grand-mère Noisette's alarm clock?

Now can you spot what time it is in each of these pictures? Answer Suzanne's question in each one by saying the time out loud in French. Use Grand-mère Noisette's alarm clock to help you with the numbers.

Word list

quelle heure est-il? keller aiteel	what time is it?
il est...heures eel ai..ur	it's...o'clock
...et demie ay demee	half past...
midi meedee	midday
minuit meenwee	midnight

You don't say *heures* after *midi* or *minuit*.

midi / minuit
meedee meenwee

onze heures
onzer

dix heures
deezer

neuf heures
neuffer

huit heures
weeter

sept heures
setter

six heures
seezer

une heure
ewn ur

deux heures
deuzer

trois heures
trwazer

quatre heures
katrer

cinq heures
sanker

Il est huit heures.

Quelle heure est-il?

A

B

C

D

E

À toi

Quelle heure est-il? [keller aiteel]. Can you say in French what time it is at the moment? Say it to the nearest half hour. If you want to say "half-past" you say *et demie* [ay demee] after the hour. To say "half-past four" you would say *quatre heures et demie* [katrer ay demee].

27

True or false?

Francine and Sophie are playing a game on the way home from school. One of them says something and the other has to say whether it is true or false.

To say, "It's true," in French, you say *C'est vrai* [sai vrai]. To say, "It's false," you say *C'est faux* [sai fo].

Can you say what the reply to each of their speech bubbles should be? Say the answers out loud. If you don't know, say *Je ne sais pas* [je ne sai pa] which means, "I don't know".

Look back through the book if you can't remember any of the words.

28   A   B   C

Word list

c'est vrai sai vrai	it's true
c'est faux sai fo	it's false
je ne sais pas je ne sai pa	I don't know
voici vwasee	here is

What's the right word?

Madame Chiffre stays late at school to correct everyone's work. Can you help her? Say out loud in French what should be written under each picture.

Voici [vwasee] means "here is". Look back through the book if you can't remember any of the words you need.

Mon livre est bleu.

Il y a trois cerfs-volants.

Mon frère s'appelle Grand-mère Noisette.

À toi

You could make your own word and picture book in French. Draw something then write what it is in French, using *voici* [vwasee] and then the name of the object. Remember to check if it is a *le* or a *la* object, so that you know whether to write *un* (for *le* words) or *une* (for *la* words) before it.

Word list

Here is a list of all the French words and phrases* used in this book in alphabetical order. Use the list either to check quickly what a word means, or to test yourself.

Cover up the English words and see if you can remember what each French word means. Do the same the other way around, covering up the French and saying the French for each English word.

The [m] or [f] after l' or les words tell you whether the word is a le word (masculine) or a la word (feminine).

à toi	ah twa	your turn
anglais (l') [m]	onglai	English
animal (l') [m]	anee mal	animal
août	oot	August
automne (l') [m]	oh tonn	autumn
avril	avreel	April
blanc, blanche	blaw, blonsh	white
bleu, bleue	bleuh	blue
bonjour	bonjoor	hello
bras (le)	bra	arm
ça va bien	sa va beeai	I'm fine
ça va très bien	sa va trai beeai	I'm very well
cadeau (le)	kado	present
cahier (le)	kaeeay	exercise book
ce n'est pas	se nai pa	it is not
ceinture (la)	santewr	belt
cerf-volant (le)	sair volaw	kite
c'est	sai	it is, that is
c'est faux	sai fo	that's false
c'est vrai	sai vrai	that's true
chapeau (le)	shapo	hat
chat (le)	sha	cat
cheval (le)	shval	horse
chien (le)	sheea	dog
cinq	sank	five
cochon (le)	ko shaw	pig
comment ça va?	kommaw sa va	how are you?
comment tu t'appelles?	kommaw tew tapell	what's your name?
content, contente	kontaw, kontont	happy
coquillage (le)	kokeeaj	shell
couleur (la)	kooler	colour
courir	kooreer	to run
crayon (le)	krayaw	pencil
de mauvaise humeur	de mo vaze ewmur	in a bad mood

décembre	daysombr	December
dessin (le)	dessa	drawing, art
deux	deuh	two
dimanche (le)	deemonsh	Sunday
dix	deess	ten
dix-huit	deezweet	eighteen
dix-neuf	deezneuf	nineteen
dix-sept	deesset	seventeen
douze	dooz	twelve
drapeau (le)	dra po	flag
école (l') [f]	aykol	school
éléphant (l') [m]	aylayfaw	elephant
elle s'appelle	el sapell	she is called
est-ce quec'est...?	ess ke sai	is it...?
et	ay	and
...et demie	ay demee	half past...
été (l') [m]	ai tai	summer
faire des cabrioles	fair day kabreeole	to do somersaults
faire la roue	fair la roo	to do a cartwheel
faire le poirier	fair le pwareeay	to do a handstand
fatigué, fatiguée	fateegay	tired
feutre (le)	feutr	felt tip pen
février	fave reeay	February
français (le)	fronsai	French
frère (le)	frair	brother
gants (les) [m]	gaw	gloves
gilet (le)	jeelay	cardigan
grand-mère (la)	gronmair	grandma
grimper	grampay	climb
hiver (l') [m]	eevair	winter
huit	weet	eight
il est ... heures	eel ai ... ur	its ... o'clock
il s'appelle	eel sapell	he is called
il y a	eel ya	there is, there are
j'ai chaud	jay show	I'm hot
j'ai faim	jay fa	I'm hungry
j'ai froid	jay frwa	I'm cold
j'ai mal à la jambe	jay mal ala jomb	my leg hurts
j'ai mal à la tête	jay mal ala tet	I have a headache
j'ai mal au ventre	jay mal oh vontr	I have a tummy-ache
j'ai mal aux dents	jay mal oh daw	I have toothache
j'ai perdu	jay pairdew	I have lost
j'ai soif	jay swaf	I'm thirsty
janvier	jonveeay	January
jardinier (le)	jardeeneeay	gardener
jaune	jone	yellow

30

*Except those in the jokes and songs which are translated on the pages or on the answer page.

je m'appelle	je mapell	I am called		plante (la)	plont	plant
je ne sais pas	je ne sai pa	I don't know		porte-monnaie (le)	port monnai	purse
je sais	je sai	I know (how to)		préféré, préférée	prai fai rai	favourite
je suis	je swee	I am		printemps (le)	prantaw	spring
jeudi (le)	jeuh dee	Thursday				
juillet	jooeeay	July		quatorze	katorz	fourteen
juin	jwah	June		quatre	katr	four
				quelle heure est-il?	keller aiteel	what time is it?
la voilà	la vwala	there she, it is		qui sait...?	kee sai	who knows (how to)...?
lapin (le)	lapa	rabbit				
le, la, les	le, la, lay	the		quinze	kanz	fifteen
le voilà	le voilà	there he, it is				
les voilà	lay vwala	there they are		ramper	rompay	to crawl
livre (le)	leevr	book		raquette (la)	rackett	racket
lundi (le)	lundee	Monday		rouge	rooj	red
lunettes (les) [f]	lewnet	glasses				
				sais-tu...?	sai tew	do you know (how to)...?
Madame	ma dam	Mrs.				
mai	may	May		salut	salew	hi
main (la)	ma	hand		samedi (le)	samdee	Saturday
marcher à cloche-pied	marshay a klosh pee ay	to hop		sauter	so tay	to jump
mardi (le)	mardee	Tuesday		seize	sez	sixteen
marelle (la)	la marell	hopscotch		sept	set	seven
marron	marraw	brown		septembre	septombr	September
mars	marss	March		sifflet (le)	seeflay	whistle
merci	mairsee	thank you		six	seess	six
mercredi (le)	mairkredee	Wednesday		sœur (la)	ser	sister
mère (la)	mair	mother		souris (la)	sooree	mouse
midi	meedee	midday		sport (le)	spor	sport
minuit	meenwee	midnight		sucette (la)	sewset	lollipop
mon, ma, mes	maw, ma, may	my				
Monsieur	miss yer	Mr.		tante (la)	tont	aunt
montre (la)	montr	watch		treize	trez	thirteen
musique (la)	mewzeek	music		triste	treest	sad
				trois	trwa	three
neuf	neuf	nine		trousse (la)	trooss	pencil case
noir, noire	nwar	black				
non	naw	no		un, une	a, ewn	a, one
novembre	novombr	November				
				vélo (le)	vaylo	bicycle
octobre	octobr	October		vendredi (le)	vondredee	Friday
oncle (l') [m]	onkl	uncle		vert, verte	vair, vairt	green
onze	onz	eleven		vingt	va	twenty
orange	oronj	orange		violet, violette	vee o lay, vee o let	purple
où est	oo ai	where is				
oui	wee	yes		voici	vwasee	here is
parapluie (le)	para plewee	umbrella		week-end (le)	weekend	week-end
pardon	pardaw	sorry				
père (la)	pair	father				
pied (le)	pee ay	foot				
pipeau (le)	peepo	recorder				

31

Answers

PAGE 4-5
This is the way Marc should go:

Here are the French answers to the questions:

Elle s'appelle Sophie.
Il s'appelle Monsieur Noisette.

PAGE 6-7
Madame Noisette should say, *J'ai mal à la jambe.*
Grand-mère Noisette should say, *Ça va très bien.*
Monsieur Noisette should say, *J'ai mal à la tête.*
Roger should say, *J'ai mal au ventre.*

PAGE 8-9
Il y a huit plantes.   *Il y a neuf crayons.*
Il y a trois parapluies.   *Il y a sept chapeaux.*
Il y a cinq cadeaux.

Here is the tune for the song:

PAGE 10-11
A. *C'est lundi.*   C. *C'est vendredi.*
B. *C'est jeudi.*   D. *C'est mardi.*

PAGE 14-15

L'éléphant (the elephant) isn't anyone's favourite.

PAGE 18-19
This is what the words mean in English:

What is it that I see there?
Is it a big old rat?
It's not a goldfish,
Nor an elephant moving,
What is it that I see there?
It's OK, it's my little cat.

PAGE 20-21
This is the way Francine should go:

PAGE 26-27
A. *Il est neuf heures.*   D. *Il est trois heures.*
B. *Il est onze heures.*   E. *Il est quatre heures.*
C. *Il est une heure.*

PAGE 28-29
A. *C'est faux.*   D. *C'est vrai.*
B. *C'est vrai.*   E. *C'est faux.*
C. *C'est faux.*   F. *C'est faux.*

Here is what should be written under each picture:
A. *Voici un chien.*   D. *Voici un crayon.*
B. *Voici un livre.*   E. *Voici mon père.*
C. *Voici un chapeau.*